Daphne, Secret Vlogger

Daphne, Secret Vlogger is published by Stone Arch Books
A Capstone Imprint
1710 Roe Crest Drive
North Mankato, Minnesota 56003
www.mycapstone.com

Library of Congress Cataloging-in-Publication Data is available on the
Library of Congress website.

Summary: A few months into the school year, Annabelle Louis is starting
to find her place at McManus Middle School. But Annabelle's therapist,
Dr. Varma, still thinks there's room for improvement in Annabelle's
social life, especially since Mom will be leaving soon for an overseas
assignment. Knowing there's a school dance coming up, Dr. Varma
challenges Annabelle to learn how to dance. What keeps Annabelle
interested in the challenge are the hilarious videos she posts on her
vlog, Daphne Doesn't, making fun of the various styles of dance she's
learning. The videos are a hit, and as Daphne Doesn't goes viral around
McManus Middle School and elsewhere, Annabelle's alter ego won't
stay secret for long. Will Annabelle continue to live a double life, or can
she find a way to combine her two identities into one?

ISBN 978-1-4965-6297-5 (library-bound hardcover)
ISBN 978-1-4965-6301-9 (paperback)
ISBN 978-1-4965-6305-7 (eBook PDF)

Cover illustration by Marcos Calo
Design by Kay Fraser

Printed and bound in Canada
PA020

DAPHNE Definitely DOESN'T DO DANCES

by Tami Charles

STONE ARCH BOOKS
a capstone imprint

Definitely doesn't do sports D

esn't do drama Definitely do

finitely doesn't do fashion D

dances Definitely doesn't do

Definitely doesn't do sports S

sn't do drama Definitely doe

finitely doesn't do fashion D

do dances Definitely doesn't

ly doesn't do sports Definitel

esn't do drama Definitely doe

finitely doesn't do fashion D

ances Definitely doesn't do F

ely doesn't do sports Definite

esn't do drama Definitely do

Definitely doesn't do Sports D

ances Definitely doesn't do F

1

LIFE = RUINED!

"My life is basically over!" I fan my face and plop myself onto Dr. Varma's couch.

Desperate times call for Academy-award winning performances! When your life feels like one big movie, this level of drama is totally appropriate.

Allow me to set the scene for you:

Outside, the sun is shining, the air is cold, and it smells like the holidays. But inside my therapist's office, I'm not feeling so merry and bright. After everything that went down these past couple of days, Dad took the liberty of calling Dr. Varma to schedule an emergency Sunday afternoon appointment.

"Oh, Annabelle, I doubt your life is over," Dr. Varma says. "Your father told me you hit a bump in the road. Why don't we start there?"

She invites me to spill it all out, so I take a deep breath and prepare for the performance of a lifetime.

The lights flash on, the camera is ready, and the imaginary film director screams, "*ACTION!*"

Welcome to the recap of the sad life that is Annabelle Louis!

Haven't heard of her? No worries! Grab your seatbelt and buckle in for the roller-coaster!

Dork by day, rising YouTube star by night, that's me!

My life as a military kid was just fine. Sure, there were a few moves—Spain, Japan, the UK, and Germany—but, at least I had my parents and best friend, Mae, in the UK to help me navigate the ups and downs.

Then, out of nowhere, Mom yanked me away from my perfect, cozy homeschool life with Dad and announced that we were moving back to the Unites States, where I was born. (Strike one!)

Next thing I knew, I was living in Linden, New Jersey, enrolling as a seventh grader at McManus Middle School, and seeing a therapist after Mom broke the news that the Air Force was sending her to Afghanistan! (Strike two!)

Dr. Varma wasted zero time giving me homework: "Make a vlog, Annabelle! It'll help you make friends and try new school activities!" (Strike three!)

Of course Mom, Dad, and Mae were one

hundred percent on Dr. Varma's side. But I couldn't go on YouTube as myself! That would be way too embarrassing! And so, my top-secret, British-accented alter ego "Daphne" was born.

Fast forward past my viral vlogs about sports, lunch, drama, and fashion, the new friends I've made (John, Clairna, and Navdeep), the enemy I've gained (*hello, Rachael Myers!*), and the fact remains that I'm STILL the biggest dork in seventh grade!

And the worst part of all? On Friday Rachael discovered my secret and threatened to tell everyone in school what a big liar I've been.

By the time I tell Dr. Varma the last part of my autobiography, I'm snot-crying through my words:

"I thought about telling John, Clairna, and Navdeep, but then I got cold feet. We were already recovering from the last blowout when I ditched them to be Rachael's friend, which was a total failure. So yesterday, I invited them over to work on the decorations for the winter ball. John wandered off to the basement, where my girl cave is—aka, where all my Daphne costumes were hidden. I rushed to find him, hoping I'd catch him before it was too late. Well, *I* was too late. He stared into my eyes for what felt like years before finally the words spilled out of my mouth: 'I can explain.'

"And you know what he said to me, Dr. Varma?"

"Do tell!" She leans in closer.

"'It's about time.'"

And cue camera zoom!

The camera view is close enough that the audience could count the number of freckles on my cheeks and the amount of tears building up in each eye—four in the left, two in the right.

Dr. Varma hands me a tissue. "So John

knew you were Daphne all along? What gave it away?"

I slump against the back of the couch. "He found my Daphne wig in the bathroom weeks before that," I explain. "Also he knew I could speak in many different accents. He even mentioned that I looked like Daphne once. And then once he saw all my Daphne costumes and the set of my vlog in my girl cave, it just confirmed everything he already suspected."

I flash back to yesterday, remembering the disappointment on John's face and the sincerity of his voice when he admitted that he knew:

"I was really mad at first," he said, "because deep down, I knew you lied. But then I talked to *abuela* about it, and she said that you probably had a good reason to not tell anyone. She said that when you were ready, you'd say something. It's not like everything about you is fake. You're still the cool girl from

Germany who can't play sports to save her life!"

I gave John a good slap on the shoulder after that.

"It's just this one small part of you that you are hiding," John said. "You will figure out the right time to let everyone else know."

I swallowed the lump in my throat after all of that.

Then John turned off the lights, shut the door to my girl cave, and walked upstairs to the dining room like nothing even happened. We ate pizza with our friends, we all had a good time, and John didn't say a word the whole night.

Dr. Varma clears her throat, snapping me out of my memory. "Have you told Clairna and Nav?"

"Not yet. I thought if I confessed then, it would ruin everything. Does that make me a bad friend?"

"Not at all. But when do you think you'll tell them?"

"Tomorrow at school. Definitely tomorrow, before Evil Queen Rachael gets to them with her big mouth."

"And what about the vlogs? Your fashion video has over fifty thousand views now. Do you think you want to continue?" Dr. Varma asks.

"At this point, I would say mission accomplished. I've made some friends, who I'd prefer not losing before Mom leaves for Afghanistan. Plus, I'm fresh out of school activities."

"Well if I heard correctly, didn't you mention that you're on the decorating committee for the winter ball? As in dance?" Dr. Varma starts up with that excitement in her voice, and I already know what she's thinking.

Here we go again!

I, Annabelle Louis, do not like sports, can't

stand drama, am a complete fashion disaster, and I definitely do not dance!

But none of that matters, because I already know what's coming next: a new vlog assignment.

2

DANCING IS NOT FOR ME

One YouTube channel. Three social experiments.

And I have hated every! Single! One!

But the numbers say otherwise: Sixty-two thousand views. Fifteen thousand subscribers.

Now Dr. Varma is extra pumped for me to keep going.

"I say you go to the winter ball, Annabelle!" she says.

I sigh, then say, "I don't dance, Dr. Varma."

"Oh, but dancing is such a useful skill to have! You will use it for the rest of your life—" Dr. Varma is interrupted by her buzzer.

She tells me to stay put and invites Dad in to tell him all about her idea for my next vlog.

"So what I'm thinking," she says, after going on and on to Dad and me about all the friends I'll make and the confidence I'll gain from trying out this new hobby, "is that 'Daphne Does Dancing' would be a wonderful vlog to end on!"

Dr. Varma claps her hands together in triumph.

To which I respond, "I change my mind. I'm not going to the winter ball anymore."

"Oh, you have to go, Annabelle! Your crush would be *crushed*," Dad says. He laughs at himself, but I don't find anything funny.

"You mean the same guy you didn't even want me hanging out with at first?" I ask.

"Oh, I like the kid. Any guy who loves his *abuela* the way John does is fine by me."

"Listen, I'm not really one for dancing either, Annabelle," Dr. Varma says. "So how about you conquer your fear of dancing by attending a class? The Linden Community Center does a free weekly social dancing class. You can even invite your friends."

I picture John, Clairna, Navdeep, and me in tutus twirling around the room and burst out laughing.

"She'll do it," Dad announces.

And just like that, I guess not only am I going to the winter ball, but I'm going to learn how to dance and share it with my YouTube followers.

Hooray.

Can't you just hear the excitement in my voice?

3

BACK AT SCHOOL

Today's mission? Find Clairna and Nav ASAP! I look for them as soon as I get to homeroom Monday morning, but they're nowhere to be found. Not even John is around. Apparently, the band will be practicing in the gym all morning. The winter ball is coming up Friday, and there isn't much time left to get all of the songs they'll be performing memorized perfectly. But I have no idea where Nav is.

Right before the first-period bell rings, Mr. Davis gets on the loudspeaker and announces: "Will the winter ball decorating committee report to the gym during lunch?"

Perfect. I'll see them then and get this confession over with once and for all!

Rachael stares at me all during homeroom, and I sit there feeling her eyes pierce holes in me, waiting for her to say something. But she doesn't.

I get through the morning periods without Rachael saying so much as one word.

The rain starts up right before lunch. No outdoor recess today, which means some students will trickle their way into the gym to hang out. I grab some of the decorations from my locker and zip down the halls to get there first.

Nav is waiting when I arrive.

"Where were you this morning? I've been looking for you," I say.

"Doctor's appointment. My parents just dropped me off. The band is just finishing up," he says, "then we can start taping the snowflakes to the walls."

I find my friends nestled among the band on stage. John is on the trumpet. Clairna is on the clarinet. She spots me and waves just as the band plays the final note of "Walking in a Winter Wonderland."

Mr. Reyes directs the band to stand up and take a bow. "Excellent work!" he says. "We'll have practice again tomorrow morning during homeroom and during first and second periods. You may be excused, but don't forget to take your instruments with you."

Then Mr. Reyes gathers his things and exits the stage. Big mistake! Kids are starting to pour into the gym and they're bringing in a lot of noise.

I see Rachael come in alone, like a one-woman show. Our eyes meet, and the slyest smile grows on her face.

Quickly, I place the box of decorations on the floor and ask Nav to follow me. I run up onto the stage, where John and Clairna are packing up their instruments.

More kids pour into the gym, a few of them bouncing basketballs.

"What'd you think of our performance, Annabelle? It was *lit*, right?" Clairna asks.

"Yeah, totally. But guys, can we go in the hallway? I want to talk to you about something."

"Oh, about the social dance class? John mentioned you wanted to invite us to it tomorrow night. I'm in!" Clairna says.

"Sounds fun . . . and embarrassing!" Nav says.

John snaps his fingers as if to say, "You better hurry up and say something!"

Rachael is drawing closer, down the aisle. And now she's got a few of her friends trickling in behind her.

"Just who I was looking for! Hello, *Daphne!*" Rachael says loudly.

The kids stop playing basketball.

Rachael's friends look at each other in pure confusion.

I scan the room for Mr. Davis, Mr. Reyes— really any teacher to magically appear and tell Rachael to shut up and for everyone else to sit quietly on the gym floor.

Of course for once there's not a teacher to be found.

Rachael's large and in charge and has everyone's attention.

She inches closer to the stage, where I'm standing with my three *amigos*, behind the microphone . . . that's apparently still on. *Thanks, Mr. Reyes.*

The sound of my pounding heart can be heard. That I am sure of.

"What did you just call her?" Clairna asks while I turn into a shriveling pile of dust.

Rachael places her hands on the stage floor and then vaults herself onto it to stand beside us. Meanwhile the crowd gathers and moves closer, eager to see the show.

"Oh, you heard correctly. I called her *Daphne.*" Then she faces the audience with her arms spread out like wings. "Ladies and gentlemen of McManus," Rachael says, "allow me to introduce you to the one, the only . . . the biggest liar in school, Daphne, YouTube star of the vlog *Daphne Doesn't!*"

Rachael is in her element now, with her shoulders rounded out and the biggest, meanest smile planted on her face. Meanwhile, my heart is pounding at top speed, and I'm looking for something, anything, to say.

The whispers from the audience begin.

"Is she for real?"

"Annabelle is a little weird . . . just like Daphne."

"They kind of look alike."

"No, they don't! Annabelle's from Germany. Daphne is British!"

My heart is in full panic attack mode. In and out, my chest heaves. John, Clairna, and Nav stand there waiting for me to say something. Clairna steps in. "You don't know what you're talking about. I watch that show, and Annabelle is nothing like Daphne!"

Then Nav steps in. "I think you're wrong about this one, Rachael. You're just trying to stir up drama, like always."

Something comes over Clairna, and she turns into someone I've never seen before. "Yeah, *girlfriend*, your braids must be too tight."

That sends the whole audience into a frenzy.

"Whoa!"

"She roasted you!"

"Can't come back from that!"

Rachael's whole face drops. She places her hands on her hips and gives Clairna the death stare.

Clairna raises her hand to slap me a high five. It's the weakest high five ever on my part.

"I'm tired of this girl thinking she can just bully people," Clairna mutters.

Rachael lifts her finger in the air, prompting everyone in the audience to shut up once again. The power this girl has, I tell you!

"Use your brains, doofuses!" she begins. "Annabelle started school a few weeks after we'd already been here. She comes from Germany and speaks all these languages, so accents probably aren't a big deal for her. And how funny is it that I caught her reciting the same lines from that 'Daphne Does Drama' video? I even heard her mom slip and call her *Daph*! And then in her last video, she wore that same necklace. . . ." Rachael looks me over frantically. "Where's the necklace, dorkface?"

Everyone is staring at me, and I can't take one more second. This is it. I have to say something . . . now.

So I step closer to Rachael, near the microphone. "Rachael is right. . . ." The whole audience gasps. "Sort of," I add. "I know Daphne."

Some of the kids in the audience start jumping and clapping. Even Clairna looks amused.

Then I add one more lie to seal the deal, "She's my cousin."

That makes everyone scream except for two people. John and Rachael.

I can't even bear to look at the disappointment on John's face. That's two strikes now.

"If Daphne the YouTube star is your cousin, prove it. Bring her to the dance. I saw the YouTube comment. She lives right here in

New Jersey!" Rachael says loud and clear on the mic.

Someone from the audience screams, "DO IT!"

Then another person joins, "DO IT!"

Next thing I know every. Single. Student. Is chanting.

"DO IT! DO IT! DO IT!"

Mr. Davis walks in from the back of the auditorium.

"Hey, what's all the commotion about?" He joins the crowd near the stage, and everyone quiets down.

"Annabelle is related to that famous YouTube star from *Daphne Doesn't!*" Clairna shouts, then she turns to me. "And holy moly, why didn't you tell me, girl?"

I don't have an answer for that, other than a shrug and a fake smile.

Rachael jumps in. "Annabelle told us that she's bringing Daphne to the winter ball."

My imaginary camera zooms in to Rachael's eyes and the special effects make them glow red. I know that Rachael is waiting for me to fall apart right there so she can prove her point and further embarrass me.

"Why, that's GREAT!" Mr. Davis yells, and everyone starts up all over again. "We can have her perform for us!"

The kids hop up onto the stage and circle me, pushing Rachael back farther and farther away from me. Her face looks angrier by the second as even her groupies surround me and hug me, saying:

"Oh my god, I can't wait to meet your cousin. This is going to be so cool."

"Annabelle, you're going to be the most popular girl in seventh grade."

"No way! Make that in the WHOLE school."

That sends Rachael stomping off the stage, down the steps, and to the double exit doors. But not a single person notices. The knots in my stomach return as I see John's face, knowing the real secret that lies between us. But for that one moment it sure does feel good to see Rachael crumble to ashes for a change.

4

MONE-WHO?

"Annabelle, come upstairs, please. We need to talk!" Dad yells as I'm hanging out in my girl cave.

That sends a shiver down my spine. I didn't tell him what happened in school today with Rachael.

"Yes, Dad."

He's sitting at the kitchen table with dinner spread out for us: pepper steak, baked potatoes topped with sour cream and chives, and a garden salad. Dad could give those chefs on the Food Network a run for their money!

"Have a seat. Let's have dinner together. I want to show you something."

The front door slams just as we dig in. Mom's been working double shifts lately, preparing for her TDY (temporary duty yonder—Air Force speak for abandon your daughter in Afghanistan for six months!).

"Smells good, Ruben. I was dreaming about your food all the way up the turnpike," Mom says. She washes her hands at the kitchen sink and joins us at the table.

Dad holds up a piece of paper. "You will never believe the email I received today about your Daphne channel."

"What is it?" I ask, confused.

"Because a number of your viewers have either watched or clicked on the ads featured in your videos, your channel has reached monetization status."

Mom starts choking on her steak and quickly reaches for water. I'm midbite, trying to translate whatever language Dad just spoke in.

"What does that mean?" I ask between chews. "Mone-who?"

Mom snatches the paper out of Dad's hand and starts breathing loudly.

"*Schätzchen, mi amor!*" Mom yelps out her German-Spanish baby talk. "It means your channel made some money, honey!"

Now I'm snatching the paper out of Mom's hand and reading through the email. My eyes dart straight to the numbers, the comma, and the ZEROS. Far more than any allowance I've ever gotten! Tension builds in my shoulders. I toss the paper away from me like it's some contagious disease.

What the heck am I supposed to do with

all of that money? Daphne was supposed to be just an experiment. I didn't ask to be viral or famous or rich!

Dad and Mom each grab one of my hands to calm me down.

"We need to talk about what to do with this money. It's not millionaire status, but at a couple thousand dollars, it's bound to keep increasing," Dad says.

"Sweetie," Mom says, "I'm not going to tell you what to do. This is your choice."

Lots of thoughts flood my brain. How am I supposed to handle all of this pressure? And my big fat lie! How am I supposed to continue to be a regular kid by day and a YouTube star by night? And now there's money involved too? I guess most kids would be screaming, *Take the money and run!* But suddenly I don't feel good anymore. I leave half of my plate uneaten, which is a first for me, especially when it comes to Dad's cooking.

"May I be excused?" I ask.

"Of course," Dad says.

I walk upstairs to my room, close the door, and drift off into a sleep where YouTube and vlogs and fans and money don't exist.

5

TOO COOL FOR TUTUS

John and Clairna are already waiting for me when I get to the community center the next night for our dance class.

"Where's Nav?" I ask.

"He texted that he couldn't make it. He forgot he had karate tonight," Clairna says.

The class is packed with a lot of people . . . old people. We're literally the youngest ones there.

The dance teacher is a tall, ballerina-thin

woman with a tight bun and a thick Russian accent.

"My name is Madame Anastasia, and today . . . we dance!" She holds her arms out in a ballet position.

"Um, Annabelle, what in the world have you signed me up for? Is this ballet?" John mutters through clenched teeth.

"Ballet is your first dance style of the night," Madame Anastasia announces. "Now, everyone, pick your shoes and tutu and let's get started!"

In front of the glass mirrors, there are two bins. One is piled high with used ballet shoes rubber banded together in pairs. The other is overflowing with tutus in pink, white, and black.

John throws his hands in the air and huffs at me, "You gotta be kidding, right?"

"Hurry along!" Madame Anastasia calls out, forcing the three of us into military stance.

I give John a look that says, "I'm super sorry."

Meanwhile Clairna snorts loud enough for the whole class to hear.

There's no turning back now. We make our way to the bins to get ballerina-fied. But the old folks beat us to the bins, taking the best and leaving behind scraps. A black tutu for Clairna, a pink one for me, and John also gets a pink tutu because it's the only one left.

My stomach rumbles with laughter as soon as he puts it on. Clairna looks ready to burst out laughing too.

And there we are: three *amigos* dressed in poofy tutus and ballet shoes, each one of us looking more ridiculous than the next.

John gives us the death stare. It doesn't take a genius to know he's thinking: *You tell anyone about this, and you will feel my wrath!*

Everyone else in the class is so serious. They're standing at the barre, stretching and warming up. We file in line to join them.

Madame Anastasia claps her hands twice, getting everyone's attention. Then she begins to pace the room as she speaks. "As many of you already know, ballet is the foundation of all social dance forms. This is why we begin tonight's class with ballet. It takes precision, technique, and—"

WHACK!

Madame taps John on the butt with her pointer.

"Oww!"

"*Posture!*" She leans into his face, and I'm sure I see her eyes glow fiery red.

Poor John! But Clairna and I are dying by this point.

Madame reviews all the ballet positions with us, first through fifth. And then she teaches us some basic moves like arabesque, pique turns, and plié.

I move through the steps in true Annabelle style: dangly, wet-noodly legs and arms that refuse to listen to anything Madame Anastasia is saying.

She says, "Feet together." My feet say, "Nice try, lady!"

No matter how hard I try, my body does the opposite.

After the twelfth posture correction, Madame Anastasia throws me a shady, "Be sure you come back again next week. We'll need lots more classes for you to get this right."

Madame Anastasia walks to the other side of the room to check on the other dancers' forms.

"I can't even begin to tell you guys how silly we look right now," I whisper through a demi-plié.

"Seriously plotting your demise right now,

Annabelle!" John grunts as he lifts on his toes to relevé.

Clairna's whole face is red now from holding in her laughter. "Trust me," she says. "We won't be doing any of these kinds of dance moves at the winter ball on Friday."

When she says the words "winter ball" I feel a twinge in my whole body.

I'm supposed to bring "Daphne" to the winter ball, and I still haven't told Clairna and Nav the truth. This tiny voice inside me says it's not the right time. I'll wait until I have them both together, in private.

"Good job, class!" Madame orders us to take off our tutus and ballet slippers. "The next style we learn is the ballroom classic waltz, a dance that requires you to be light on your feet and move with grace! Now, partner up!"

Everyone finds a partner except me.

There are an odd number of students in the class.

Madame Anastasia comes over to us and says, "You three will work together. You, sir," she says to John, "begin with her." She points to Clairna.

Madame shows the class the moves and counts. "Sway your body to the left! Point your toes forward! Don't forget to end in the promenade position!"

For me it goes in one ear and out the other.

When Madame tells us to switch partners, Clairna says, "This will be good practice for you. Rachael is going to be so jealous when she sees you dancing like the belle of the ball. I can't wait to see the look on her face."

My stomach makes this loud gurgling noise, but then Madame Anastasia turns on the music, which thankfully covers up the sound.

"How much longer before you tell her that you're really Daphne?" John whispers.

"I need more time," I say, stepping on his toes.

"Ouch!"

"Sorry about that," I say.

My feet turn outward like a duck's, and I try my best to keep up with John, who is clearly much better at this waltz thing than I am.

"Well, don't take too long."

For the final dance, Madame says she has a guest teacher who will show us how to do hip-hop line dances.

"Ladies and gentlemen, I introduce to you master hip-hopper, JT!"

The whole class goes wild when this guy walks in. If I didn't know any better, I'd think he was on one of those dance shows I've seen on television.

JT says we'll learn three line dances: the Cha-Cha Slide, the Wobble, and the Dougie.

But first he shows us the moves for each dance.

Boom boom, kat, ske dee dow!

That's literally how he teaches the moves. No counting. Just shouting out these words as he dips and slips and slides in front of us.

To me, none of it makes any sense. But John and Clairna already know all the moves. They have both done these dances plenty of times at weddings and birthday parties.

The music begins, and the singers tell us what to do—sort of. Slide to the left, slide to the right.

But everything is going so fast, and I start bumping into the other dancers. Meanwhile everyone is getting down with their bad selves like a bunch of professional back-up dancers!

Two hours later, the torture—I mean *dance class*—is finally over.

Yet another meaningless experiment brought on by Dr. Varma. I'm starting to think this woman doesn't know what she's doing.

6

DAPHNE VLOGS ABOUT DANCING

As soon as I get home, I retreat to my girl cave. The whole world needs to know just how pointless dancing is.

I throw on an outfit from the clothing rack, along with an orange wig styled in a bun, and a *Phantom of the Opera* mask. I look fabulously ridiculous.

I blast a playlist of Beyoncé, Demi Lovato, and Lady Gaga, and let the music take over. Going live in *three . . . two . . . one . . .*

"Hey, guys. It's your girl, Daphne, and I'm here with your latest episode of *Daphne Doesn't*. Today's topic? Dancing. Here are the top five reasons I definitely don't dance:

"Number one: It's just awful. Yeah, I said it. Sorry, not sorry! People moving and sweating and bumping into each other? Not for me!

"Number two: My school is having a dance, and honestly, I don't want to go. I don't want to be at school for a minute longer than I have to be. Not only do I have to wake up early to go to school and work hard all day, I'll have to come home, shower, and change into some itchy, cutesy outfit, just to go back to school and hug the wall for three more hours. Why? Because I CAN'T dance! No thanks. I'd rather stay home.

"Number three: Line dances are the WORST! My poor dance teacher tried his best to teach me how to become a professional "Dougie-ist," but that was an epic fail. I'm sorry, but people look silly trying to do the

Dougie. And don't get me started on the Wobble!

"Number four: The Cha-Cha Slide has WAY too many instructions! Slide to the left? Slide to the right? Drop it to the floor and try not to break your knees getting up? It's bad enough that I have to listen to instructions all day at school! I'll save myself the torture and stay away from the dance floor!

"Number five: Last but not least, I'd like to go on record saying that ballet is the most evil of all dance forms! The expectation compared to the reality is way off! Expectation? You're dressed in your pretty tutu with your perfect ballerina bun, doing the most perfect grand jeté! Reality? You look like a sweaty dog, leaping for a Frisbee while playing in the park with your human.

"So there you have it, people. The top five reasons why I definitely don't dance. Sure, it's easy to say that with a little effort, and maybe even a few dance classes, anyone can learn how to dance. I don't agree with this at all. I think dancing is a natural ability. It's probably best to acknowledge when you're just not good at something so you can make the time to find what you're really good at. Which in my case is NOT dancing!"

The drum beat kicks in louder. I throw my leg high in the air, try my best to do a grand jeté leap, and tumble down to the floor.

"See what I mean? Don't forget to like, share, subscribe, and comment."

The love pours in throughout my live video:

LizaBooxoxo: This might be your funniest video yet.

CheerTay245: You might have given yourself a concussion with that last dance move. That's why I don't dance either!

OfficialNena13: Daphne is coming to my school dance! It's going to be LIT!

7

BLAST FROM THE PAST

Ever since the Daphne announcement, the other students have been following me everywhere I go. And when I say everywhere, I mean *every*where.

They're at my locker, stuffing themselves at our lunch table—not even complaining about its proximity to the garbage can—and this one kid had the nerve to slip a note under my stall door while I was using the bathroom: *So do you think you can get your cousin to autograph this for me?*

It was a crumpled-up tissue. I didn't stay long enough to see if the boogers came included.

Between that and the constant "How does it feel to be related to someone famous?" comments, I think I've had enough.

And apparently, so has Rachael. Her queen status has been demoted.

When the dismissal bell rings, I dart out of the front doors, searching for Mom's car. It just so happens that Rachael is walking out the front doors at the same time. She looks at me but doesn't say anything. Everyone else is rushing out to the busses, but not her.

"You're not taking the bus today?" I ask her.

"Don't try to be nice to me now," she snaps.

We both stop walking and face each other while hundreds of students race out of the school like it's on fire.

"Me? You're the one who started all of this drama!" I say.

"Well, all you had to do was admit the truth. Instead you just made the lie bigger and made me look like a liar, when really *you're* the liar." Rachael rolls her eyes, but then gazes past me. "Wait. Why is my mom talking to your mom?"

I whip my head around, and sure enough there are our two moms, hugging each other by their cars.

Rachael and I race past the students and the buses to intervene.

"Mom, we gotta hurry up and go," Rachael says nervously.

"Umm, yeah, me too. Mom, let's get out of here," I say.

"Rachael, don't be so rude. Put your things in the car and come meet an old friend of mine!"

Rachael tosses her backpack into the car, slams the door shut, and walks to the driver's side, where both our moms are standing. Mom gives me a look that says, *you'd better get yourself over here too.*

I take a deep breath and follow Rachael, nervous smile and all.

Mom starts, "Rachael, I didn't know that your mom was the one and only Sharon Wright, Linden High Basketball star!"

Rachael's mom whips her dreadlocks to the side and starts laughing. "Hey now!"

"So you two went to school together?" I ask.

"Nice to meet you, Annabelle, and we sure did!" Rachael's mom holds out her hand for me to shake it.

Rachael coughs and says "Daph" under her breath. No one catches it but me.

"It's good to meet you too, Mrs. Myers," I say.

"Oh, it's back to Ms. Wright." Rachael's mom then mutters to mine, "The divorce was finalized last year."

Rachael shrinks about three inches toward the ground. That's when I do the math in my head. She told me her dad was deployed almost a year ago. The divorce must have happened around the same time. Talk about a double whammy!

"I'm sorry to hear about that. You and Mike were Linden High's magic couple," Mom says.

"Well, sometimes the magic doesn't last. But you know what? I'm real glad to see you back in Linden after all these years. Now our girls can grow up together and be the best of friends like we were."

I gulp an imaginary sip of shame juice. By the looks of it, Rachael's drinking from the same cup. The last word we'd probably use for each other right about now is "friend."

"Let's not speak in past tense anymore," Mom says. "We gotta reconnect, girl. And hopefully sooner than later because I'm leaving after Christmas for a six-month assignment in Afghanistan."

Now I'm the one shrinking to the ground, because for the past three months I've tried to wipe away that thought. Pretend that the moment will never come, even though time is flying.

Ms. Wright gasps, reaches for me, and pulls me in for a hug.

"Oh, we're gonna look out for your baby girl while you're gone. You have our word. Right, Rachael?" Everyone's eyes shift to Rachael, who nods reluctantly.

"I really appreciate that, Sharon," Mom says.

"It's too bad you guys didn't move here last year. Rachael had it bad when her dad first left. Changed her whole attitude!"

"Mom!" Rachael says, flames flying from her mouth.

But Ms. Wright just swings her hand in the air and pays Rachael no attention.

"Deployment can be hard on children, I know. That's why we've been taking Annabelle to see a therapist to help her prepare for my trip."

Now I'm the one saying, "Mom!"

"Oh hush, there's nothing wrong with being able to express your feelings."

"You got that right!" Ms. Wright and Mom link their hands together.

"There was this camp I wanted to send Rachael to last summer. It's just for military kids whose parents have been or are currently deployed. But with everything that went on with the divorce and finding a new place to live, the expense was too much."

By now, I see water forming in Rachael's eyes. And she looks nothing like the cool, fashion-savvy, diva leader of McManus that I'm used to seeing. The girl standing next to me is . . . empty.

I understand now. The mood swings. The

teasing. The random moments of sadness. The deployment. The effort to put on a brave face and pretend like everything is perfect, when in reality, nothing is.

And there's that tug in my stomach again. And that curious voice that wonders what I could do to change all of that for Rachael, but also for me too.

Without anyone seeing, I take my index finger and poke Mom on the arm.

Code for: "I need to leave now."

Also code for: "I need some time to think through my feelings."

Dr. Varma would be proud that I haven't spontaneously combusted.

Mom gives Ms. Wright a hug. "Let me get this girl home so she can get her homework done. I'll see you at the winter ball?"

Ms. Wright says that she'll be attending the ball with Rachael. The four of us part ways and head to our cars.

Mom starts the engine and turns the heat

on. "What a blast from the past, huh?" she says.

"Mom . . ."

"Yes?"

"I can do whatever I want with that YouTube money?"

"Whatever you want."

8

TEXTING MAE
IN THE UK

As soon as I get home, I blast through my homework—twenty fraction word problems and a reader's response sheet to the Langston Hughes poem, "Dreams."

I get a notification on my phone from YouTube. My last video, "Daphne Definitely Doesn't Dance" hit one hundred fifty thousand views! In my mind, I see the dollar signs adding up.

Most kids would be pumped about this,

but not me. If I've learned nothing else from Dr. Varma's social experiments, it's that I couldn't care less about being rich or famous.

I wrap up my homework and start searching the Internet to flesh out my plan. It doesn't take long to find what I'm looking for. Everything I need is right there. The information, the person in charge, and the contact phone number.

My phone beeps again. It's a text from Mae. Perfect timing. I tell her all about my plan for the YouTube money, and I can hear her scream her response right through the text:

Mae: Really? Are you sure that's what you want? You're a much better person than me!

Me: It's the right thing to do.

Mae: Well since you're in the mood

for surprises, I'll have one for you real soon.

Me: What is it??? The suspense is killing me!

Mae: You'll just have to wait a little longer, *amiga*!

I finish up my texting with Mae, shut down the lights in my girl cave, and head upstairs to have dinner with Mom and Dad.

Dad strikes again with another chef-quality meal: crab-stuffed salmon, garlic mashed potatoes, and steamed broccoli. My lips are dragging on the floor by the time I reach the table.

Halfway through dinner I announce, "I surfed the Internet and found what I was looking for. This is what I want to do with the money."

Then I slide the printout across the table to my parents for them to take a look. They sit in silence reviewing the paper.

"How much?" Dad grabs his glass to take a sip of water.

"All of it," I respond.

Dad almost chokes.

Mom smiles and fights back her tears. "That's my girl."

9

THE DRAMA RETURNS

It's the day before the dance. Nav, John, Clairna, and I decide to meet in the auditorium during recess to put the finishing touches on the decorations. The final piece we have to make is the blue and white balloon arch.

We blow up so many balloons, and with each one I feel the tension creeping up in my shoulders.

It's just the four of us in the auditorium.

Mr. Davis ran to the office to make some copies.

"I don't care how weird I look dancing tomorrow. I'm gonna dance the night away." Nav does some robotic move, and John and Clairna start laughing.

"I'm so excited. Mom's pulling me out of school a little early so I can get my hair and nails done. What are you gonna wear, Annabelle?" Clairna asks.

This is the moment I've been waiting for. "I'm dressing up . . . as Daphne." I say the last two words almost like a whisper.

Nav leans in. "Like who?"

"Why would you want to dress up like your cousin?" Clairna fills a balloon with air.

"She's not," John says.

The balloon slips from Clairna's lips and swirls all the way to the floor.

"Not what? Not coming?" Nav looks at John for answers.

John shakes his head. "My name is Bennett, and I ain't in it." He continues to place the balloons on the arch.

"I've been lying to you guys," I say.

Clairna's jaw drops lower with the passing of each second. Nav just kind of stands there looking like he doesn't know what to do with his arms.

"Girl, I am not following you. So your cousin isn't coming?" She snaps her fingers together. "Darn, I *so* wanted to rub that in Rachael's face!"

I scan my brain for the right words. "No, it's just that—Daphne is . . . *me*."

Nav doubles over and starts laughing. "So you're your own cousin? What kind of freaky joke are you trying to tell?"

John finally stops building the arch and throws me an anchor. "Guys, what Annabelle is trying to say is that her real name is Annabelle *Daphne* Louis. She's Daphne, the YouTube star."

Clairna and Nav don't say anything for a second, but it doesn't take long for Clairna to show how she really feels about my keeping a secret.

"You've been lying to us this whole time?" Her voice is a good three pitches higher than before.

"Why didn't you just tell us from the beginning?" Nav says. Then he looks at John, disappointment all over his face. "And you kept it from us too?"

"Wait, you told John before you told me? I thought I was your girl, Annabelle!" Red surfaces on Clairna's whole face.

"This isn't John's fault," I say. "He was just trying to be a good friend."

"Well, that makes one of us!" Clairna says.

"I can explain," I say. "All of this was an experiment to try new things at school as a way to make friends, since I was new here."

"So that's what we are to you, *Daphne*?

An experiment?" The words jump out of her mouth like a pack of knives.

"You guys aren't an experiment. You were the first friends I made here. It's just that once I started getting popular, I felt like if I said anything about the YouTube thing you wouldn't want to be my friends anymore."

"Well, you got that part right!"

"Are you gonna tell?" I ask.

"You can have your experiments and your fans and your lies! I'm sure you'll figure out how to let everyone else down." Clairna storms out of the auditorium, and Nav runs after her.

And my tears start up all over again. "What am I supposed to do now?"

John hands me a tissue from his pocket. The tears are coming out thick and fast. I wipe my eyes with it, trying my best to stop the flow, but it doesn't work.

"Now you find a way to tell the truth . . . to everyone."

"But how?" I ask.

John scratches a patch of hair on his head, but doesn't offer a response.

"I understand if you don't want to be my friend anymore either," I say.

John places his hand on my shoulder. "I'm not going to let you go through all of this by yourself."

"But everyone is expecting me to show up tomorrow with my cousin Daphne. Clairna and Nav hate me. Rachael hates me. Meanwhile thousands of people in YouTube land think I'm the greatest thing ever, but those people aren't real. You guys are. Basically this whole experiment is one big failure."

Just then Mr. Davis walks in, in the best mood ever.

"Tomorrow is the big day, guys!" he shouts. "Ah, it looks like a winter wonderland in here!" He skips and sings his way up to the stage where we're standing.

I turn my back so he doesn't see the red in my eyes.

John says, "We're all done with decorations, Mr. Davis. If you don't mind, we'll head back to class."

I look around the gym. It's done, but it's not to my full liking. But none of that matters because I don't have the energy to blow up one more balloon.

"Where are we going?" I ask John.

"Do you have your cell phone and your laptop on you?"

"Yeah, but why?"

"You're going to the dance tomorrow . . . as Daphne. It's time for one final experiment."

10

A REASON TO SMILE

Mae: How does Christmas with your BFF sound?

Me: What are you talking about?

Mae: Effective Monday, the Tanakas are taking on the Big Apple, New York City. We'll be on holiday for two weeks!

Me: STOPPPP!

Mae: So you don't want to see me?

Me: Wait, no! Omg. Of course I do! This is the best news I've heard all year.

Mae: You ready for the dance tonight, *amiga*?

Me: Ready as I'm gonna be.

11

THIS IS IT

Mom helps me get dressed for the dance. I choose a Victorian-style winter white dress with lace and ruffles, along with a white and silver wig and the mask from my last video.

"I think you're doing the right thing, sweetie. I'm so proud of you, Annabelle," Mom says as she brushes blush on my cheeks.

Dad knocks on the door and peeks his

head in. "John and his *abuela* are here," he says.

When I get to the stairs, John is waiting for me at the bottom, standing next to his grandmother. In his hands he holds two rose corsages. It's like a scene straight out of Cinderella. John is dressed in a black suit with a silver tie to match my silver and white wig.

"*¡Tan lindos!*" his grandmother squeals, calling the two of us beautiful.

I glide down the stairs, and John places one corsage on my wrist and then one on his grandmother's wrist. Then he takes a bow.

"Are we ready for a fun night?" he asks.

"I hope so!" I shrug my shoulders.

Mom and Dad grab their coats, and we all head to the car.

McManus is lit up on the outside with holiday lights, and the streets are full of parked cars. People are standing out in the cold, with signs in their hands that say, "Welcome to McManus, Daphne!"

I want to scream and tell Mom to turn the car around and drive us back home and apologize to John's *abuela* for ruining what supposed to be a "night out on the town" for her. But I can't say any of it. Not now. Seeing the excitement on John's face, I try to ignore the fear I feel.

The flashing lights blind me as soon as I step out of the car.

"Whoa, I wasn't expecting all of this!" Dad jumps out of the passenger side and comes around to grab me. He takes his arm and wraps it around me while people are screaming:

"Oh my goodness! Look! It's Daphne, guys!"

We push our way through the crowd with Mom, John, and his *abuela* sticking close behind us.

When we finally get in, I see Mr. Davis waiting for us. He gets all excited and says, "Welcome to McManus, Daphne! We're so lucky to have you here at the McManus Student-Parent Winter Ball. Say, where's your cousin Annabelle?"

Everybody is silent, looking at me.

I clear my throat and throw on my British accent.

"Well I . . ."

"Oh, no worries! Knowing Annabelle, she's probably checking to make sure the decorations are to her liking. I tell you, Mr. and Mrs. Louis, your daughter is quite the perfectionist!"

Dad and Mom flash Mr. Davis their best smiles.

"We're going to open the doors soon and get the party started. But first I want to make sure that you have everything you need, John. You mentioned something about the projector screen?" Mr. Davis asks.

John's eyes grow wide. "Yes! Let me make sure everything is set up now before you open the doors."

"Ooh, are we going to see a new episode of *Daphne Doesn't?*" Mr. Davis asks.

John and I look at each other.

"Um, something like that," I say.

Mom, Dad, and John's *abuela* make their way to the snack and punch table in the back of the gym.

I follow John backstage to help him set up.

The band members are let in early, along with Mr. Reyes. I see Clairna walk in just as John readies himself to join the band and leave me alone backstage. Clairna is wearing a red velvet dress with a black belt and black shoes. Her hair is styled in big cluster curls with a Santa hat to complete the look.

She. Looks. Amazing.

"I'll come back here when it's time. Will you be OK?" John asks.

"Sure," I say, though I'm not sure one bit.

Then John does the strangest thing. He hugs me. For five seconds longer than a *that's-just-my-buddy* level hug. I don't know what to do with my hands. Wrap them around his back? His neck? How do they do it in those teen rom-com movies again? It's all too much to think about, so I just stand there with my arms dangling at my sides until the moment is over.

He pulls away, winks at me, and then takes his position on stage with the rest of the band. Mr. Davis starts to open the doors. The band plays "Walking in a Winter Wonderland" as the students run into the gym, screaming, with their parents trailing behind them. A few more songs—"Deck the Halls" and "Jingle Bells"—and their performance is complete.

"Ladies and gentlemen, boys and girls, let's hear it for the McManus Middle

School band!" Mr. Davis announces on the microphone.

Just then, I see Nav enter the gym with his parents. Then Rachael and her mom. I'm behind the curtains so she doesn't see me, but I can already tell who she's looking for . . . Daphne.

The DJ starts to play "I've Got a Feeling" and everyone heads to the dance floor. Halfway through the song, the kids start chanting: "DAPHNE! DAPHNE! DAPHNE! DAPHNE!"

Mr. Davis runs to the stage and taps the microphone. "Is this thing on?"

The DJ lowers the music.

Everyone starts cheering wildly.

"I believe this is the moment we've all been waiting for," Mr. Davis says. "The whole school's been buzzing about our guest of honor all week. Let's bring up two very special ladies to the stage: McManus's very own Annabelle Louis and her cousin, Daphne, the YouTube star of the hit vlog *Daphne Doesn't!*"

I inhale a deep breath in the middle of everyone screaming and take one step, then another, and another. Soon I emerge from behind the curtain.

Everyone is clapping except Rachael, Clairna, and Nav, who I spot right away in the crowd.

I clear my throat, prepare myself to speak as Daphne, and the whole auditorium quiets down. But they're all turning their heads toward each other, as if to ask, "Where is Annabelle?"

"Thank you, Mr. Davis. I thought for days and days about what I would say in this moment, standing in front of all of you, the students, teachers, and community members of McManus Middle School. Every time I went to write the words down, I balled up the paper and tossed it in the recycling. The truth is, for me to really speak my mind, I had to do what I do best . . . make a vlog."

Someone screams, "Oh my goodness, sneak preview!"

"So without further ado, I present to you my latest and final vlog. I call this episode 'Daphne Tells the Truth.'"

Now everyone is looking confused.

John lowers the house lights and presses play. An image of me sitting in the paper supply closet fades in.

"I know you guys were probably expecting to see Daphne in her full fabulous gear, but I have a confession to make. The girl you've been watching on YouTube isn't real. She's a made-up persona, just created by a regular dorky girl who was trying to make friends. Allow me to introduce myself. My name is Annabelle Daphne Louis."

Everyone gasps.

"And I've been lying this whole time. I owe everyone a big apology, but especially my best friends here at McManus—John, Clairna, and Navdeep. I never meant for this social experiment to grow out of control. I didn't want to be famous. All I wanted were friends to turn to when my mom leaves with the Air Force to Afghanistan. But things got out of hand, and next thing I knew I was doing any and everything I could to cover it up. I didn't want any fame or fortune out of my YouTube channel, but I couldn't stop it from happening.

"So effective immediately, the *Daphne Doesn't* vlog is canceled. The money I've made from it will be donated to a good cause. I'm sorry if I hurt anyone, and I understand if no one ever wants to be my friend again."

The video fades to black.

John raises the houselights, and there's a sea of frozen, shocked faces staring back at me.

I remove the wig and let my poofy, curly

hair do what it does best—find its way toward the ceiling.

"So there you have it," I say into the microphone in my normal voice. "I am Annabelle Daphne Louis. Shy, sometimes funny, dorky, and proud of it. I don't do sports. I don't do drama. I don't do fashion. And if you saw my last vlog, you know that I definitely don't dance."

The crowd cuts me off with laughter.

"But here is what I love doing: being with my friends, doing cool things with my video camera and computer, and spending time with my family, especially my mom . . . who I am going to miss very, very much when she goes overseas."

I'm fighting back the single tear that's building up in my left eye. And then the strangest thing happens. Clairna starts clapping. Then Nav. Then Rachael shouts, "It's OK, Annabelle!" And one by one, the others join in.

I place my hands over my mouth to stop myself from crying yet again. Mom rushes to the stage to hug me, along with Mr. Fingerlin, the school counselor, who steps up to the microphone.

"The Louis family has a special presentation."

Mom speaks next. "Thank you, Pete. My daughter, Annabelle, is the kindest person I know. She did her research and found a wonderful organization to donate her earnings to. My husband and I contacted them and asked for a representative to be here tonight.

"Will Mr. Barry Ellis please come to the stage to receive a donation of three thousand dollars to the Military Kids United Camp?"

I see Rachael's face light up at the sound of that.

A tall man with a bald head and glasses walks up to receive the check. We take pictures for the newspaper, the *Linden Leader*. Every single person in the audience is clapping, and they keep clapping through Mr. Ellis's speech.

"I can't thank the Louis family enough for their generosity to donate money to our organization and for choosing to sponsor several well-deserving children to attend our camp next summer.

"Military Kids United serves all children of members of our armed forces, but especially those children whose parents are deployed. Our organization provides a summer of fun for these kids. We take them swimming, hiking, and on trips to experience new cultures and sights. We do all that we can to make sure that while our military is off protecting our freedom, their children are here in the United States, enjoying theirs.

"So once again, I say thank you, and I encourage Miss Annabelle to not give up on her YouTube channel. As you can see, the people love it. But I do have one suggestion. I know *Daphne Doesn't* is a funny way of talking about all the things you don't do. How about renaming it to *Annabelle Always* and posting videos about being true to the things you love? What do you think, audience?"

The crowd goes wild and starts screaming, "YES!"

I step forward and say, "That sounds like a good idea, sir."

John dims the houselights again. Mr. Davis screams in the microphone, "Let's continue the party, guys!"

The beat picks up, loud and proud. On my way down the stage stairs, people are patting me on the back, telling me I did a good job, and asking for selfies.

Outside of the big windows, the snow starts falling, letting everyone know that winter has made its entrance into Linden.

I feel a tap on my back. I turn around and see that it's Rachael. "I'm really—" I start.

"I think you've apologized enough for one day, Annabelle," she says. "That was really cool what you did—donating to the camp like that. And that's cool that you chose to sponsor some campers next summer. Those kids are really lucky."

"Yeah, I know. You're gonna love it!" I say, and I feel a smile wrap around my whole face.

Rachael's eyes double in size. "Are you saying what I think you're saying?"

"I can't wait to hear all about it . . ." I trail off. "That is, if you want to tell me. You don't have to. I understand that I messed up."

"Oh, shut up! You stop it right now!" Rachael grabs me hard and pulls me in for a hug.

"I heard your mom say that you wanted

to go to that camp, but with everything your family was going through, it wasn't going to work out."

"Yeah, things have been hard between the divorce and the deployment. And I know I wasn't so nice to you. Can we start over?"

I hold out my hand to shake hers. "Friends?"

"Definitely."

Mom and Ms. Wright dance their way over to us.

The song "True Friend" by Miley Cyrus comes on. John, Clairna, and Nav find their way to Rachael and me.

No words are spoken. No further apologies are necessary.

We just start dancing to the beat, like old friends. Make that new ones. Because starting right here and right now, everything is brand-new again. This city. This school. These friends.

I dance my dorky heart out and whisper a wish to the sky. Six months will fly, but Mom will come back. And I've got the best "squad" around to help me get through it all.

TALK ABOUT IT!

1. Clairna and Nav are upset when they find out Annabelle was lying to them. How do you think they would have reacted if they'd known Annabelle was Daphne earlier?

2. Annabelle's videos become monetized, and she makes more money than she ever thought she would from them. How do you think she felt about the sudden amount of money? How would you feel?

3. Rachael's mom tells Annabelle that Rachael has had a hard time since her parents were divorced and her dad was deployed. Do you think Annabelle sympathizes with Rachael? Why or why not?

WRITE IT DOWN!

1. Annabelle lies when Rachael tells a crowd of classmates that she's Daphne, and claims that Daphne is her cousin. Write about why you think she lies to the crowd instead of telling the truth.

2. No matter what she's going through, Mae is always Annabelle's friend. Imagine you're Annabelle and write a thank-you letter to Mae.

3. Mr. Davis suggests Annabelle make a new series called *Annabelle Always* and talk about things she *likes* doing. Write your own script for an *Annabelle Always* post and talk about something you like to do.

ABOUT THE AUTHOR

Tami Charles writes picture books, middle grade and young adult fiction, and nonfiction. Her middle grade novel debut, *Like Vanessa*, is a Junior Library Guild selection. *Like Vanessa* was also selected by the American Bookseller's Association for the Indies Introduce Kids List. Tami is the author of four more books forthcoming with Albert Whitman & Co., Candlewick, and Charlesbridge. She resides in New Jersey with her husband and son.